- A Novel by Zaire Hodges

The Blue House on the Left

A Novel by Zaire Hodges

Cover created and designed by: Jazzy Kitty Publishing

Logo designs by: Andre M. Saunders and Leroy Grayson

Editor: Anelda Attaway

© 2013 Zaire Hodges

ISBN: 978-0-9892656-7-6

PROLOGUE

After my debut novel, I had decided to take a different direction. The year that I was getting it published, I had been listening to audio books where the writers had a male character that was mainly young teenage boys. That month I was listing to an audio book, titled Sapphires the Kid, and I liked how she had her male character Abdul think everything in real life. Therefore, I sat down and decided that it was time for me to create a book with a male character. My own creation, but of a fictionalized person. Therefore, I did just that. I created the character and called him Javio Martez. He is my creation showing just about almost everything that can truthfully happen to one person or many people's lives. So enjoy the book.

The Blue House on the Left – A Novel by Zaire Hodges

ACKNOWLEDGMENTS

I want to thank everyone who has supported me just like I support them. Love all you guys.

To my Mom that supports all my stories as realistic or crazy as they maybe be. Thank You So Much! Love You.

Thanking God for all my blessings a million times.

Thank you too, the publishing company for their help, kindness, and support. Also, for making me less nervous to write about different stories on world events.

DEDICATIONS

To: God for laying it on my heart to tell a story that will help many people.

To: People who are currently struggling with addiction, and those who have beat addiction.

To: Jazzy Kitty Publishing for being willing to publish this raw uncut piece of realistic fiction. Thank you.

To: My Reading teachers who helped me day in and day out editing my work. Thank you so much!

This book is not about anyone I know; it is an art of realistic fiction of things that can really happen, and turning a negative into a positive.

To: MTV for airing Dr. Drew Celebrity Rehab, I watched it since the first season. I want to thank MTV for putting it on their network. It helped me understand and clearly see what can happen, and the hopeful outcome.

TABLE OF CONTENTS

TABLE OF CONTENTS

INTRODUCTION

The novel The Blue House on the Left, is about a young man who is Brazilian and Puerto Rican who has to move from Brazil. He moves to New York City in 1975 when he is five years old while dealing with both his temperamental and ruff father, and a caring but serious mother.

A few years later in 1985, he is 15 years old dealing with serious personal issues. How will his life pan out? Find out in The Blue House on the Left - A Novel by Zaire Hodges.

CHAPTER 1

Home Life

I am walking the streets, and my feet shuffle as if I am so cool; like I am the man, the big guy whom everybody wants to be. But I'm not; I am just me, Javio Martez, a teenage boy from Brazil.

We are moving to New York, and I think I repeat my mother's words inside my head, Nueva York, she says. I walk back up towards the house; I will miss the house, and I thought to myself...*mi casa es de color azul,* which means my house is blue. My mother drilled Spanish in me; she speaks both Espanola (Spanish) and English. She says she wants me to be well rounded.

My dad is just my dad, not too much to say. Except he can get upset and mad easily, and he always does something to make my mother upset and hissing angry. Nevertheless, she just puts up with it anyway. But she's not stupid; she does stand up for herself and for me.

One time my dad got mad and shocked me like a rag doll; like the ones that little girls play with. He said loudly, "Be a man, damn it...be a man!" Why I thought I was? I had not done anything sissy like, so why was I less of a young man? I could barely see him with my eyes shaking and rolling around like small-doted Mar balls. In addition, having his hand smack me on the face. I just looked in shock, like asking who is this man? In anger, he pushes me on the bathroom floor, which has pretty white tile, and some blood from my hand falls on the tile like a snowfall. As I am staring at it, my mother gets up and punches my father in the face. He grabs his nose, and his nose is bleeding. He is fuming mad now. I can hear the heavy breathing coming from him, and I twitch at the sound. He grabs her by her hair, and she spits in his face. He turns his face in discuss, and let her go. Then he walks out of the bathroom, and out the house still mad. My mother cleans me up with hot water and a rag. When she places the rag on my face, it stings like a needle pinching or an astray that was touched. My mother kisses me on the forehead, and takes me to an orange farm down the road.

When we arrived at the farm, we ate the juicy oranges in silence. The only sound you hear is us sucking the juice out of them. Even though the only time we had laughed was when I had, all the tan seeds on my red shirt spilled all over it. My mother looked up at me and laughed with my eyes wandering like little black dots. She loves them so much, and she says your eyes tell your heart. Even now, when I stand and look up at her with my tall fifteen-year old frame, she still stares into my eyes. And when I think about the oranges, it is one of my best memories in the blue house, my house. Maybe it's the only one.

That all happened when I was? Well...when I was five in 1975. Now I am here in 1985, fifteen in New York City. We moved to Brooklyn two months ago before we scattered around New York. But, we finally settled here in Brooklyn. We live among the Blacks and Spanish; that's the area that we live in. It's nice so far for me, in my option. We live on the fourth floor in an apartment complex next to a store. That was the first thing that my mother was thankful for, she said to me, "Oh my Hijo, there is a store." She seemed giddy with excitement over the smallest things, and wanted me Hijo meaning her son, to see it as if it was new and never existed.

I guess that's just how my mother Rosie is because when she grew up, she never got to fetcher out to other areas of her hometown. I just think it's a part of her. I can tell that she likes it here, and she has her friends too. Marta is a Spanish lady, and Lorraine is a Black lady. They sit outside and talk to my mother every day-after work. She likes them, and she says that they're her friends. I am glad she likes it.

She has a good job too; she is a typist for the New York Post. I bag about how proud I am of her, and her great job at school. My dad's job is to do work at a cleaner's downtown in Times Square. My mother validates my father's job but says it's just basic, and he hates doing it, but he pretends he likes it. She tells me to do something you love and not something you're forced. Like in the case of my father who does not have a high school diploma like my mother does. Her family and her father Tito Chavez valued education and inspired her to go to classes and school. At times, I think my mother thinks she's better than him, which I learned from others it is not a nice quality to have. I feel bad for him sometimes.

CHAPTER 2

New York City

My hair is jet-black, and I am swiping it aside my face. I brush it; I've got a 1950s style cut...a Fedora that's what I got. I am looking at myself in the mirror with my white shirt on. I play around trying to flex my muscles looking at my light caramel colored skin. Flexing is funny, and my boxers are showing my legs to be strong the way they are now, and not flimsy like when I was eight makes me proud. I am no longer that flimsy skinny elementary school kid. I am me, a tall muscled fifteen years old. I put on my clothes, my white muscular shirt, jeans, and black shoes. Then I put on my red sports jacket with the white sides to it on my body and walked out to the kitchen.

When I get to the kitchen, I greet my mother, and she smiles happily. However, my dad looks at me stern, and then I said, "Hey dad." Then I leave it alone. He just nods, and I eat my oatmeal with blue berries that my mother made; I love her food. I ate the oatmeal and then drank orange juice. Then it is time to go; it's Saturday.

My mother drives me every day to school to my class because she says she is nervous that I will get jacked, as they call it. She says Chico meaning boy. "Chico, someone just had that happened, I wrote about it in a column that's why I drive you," she said, and then she kisses me on the check, "go play." She rushes me off, so I go out to the park in our area, and I dribbled the basketball for thirty minutes. Then I went back inside because there is no one outside.

Therefore, I said I will watch basketball. However, my mother says, "Don't start to watch basketball your dads at work, so the TV is mine." My dad works three days, Friday, Saturday, and Sunday. He does that because he said men work hard, but I think the real reason is to prove my mother wrong, and get a break from her. While drinking a soda, I yelled at the TV, "Past the ball jerk face!" My mother giggles at me yelling.

Last night as I ate my green beans, mashed potatoes' and yellow rice, and my mother said, "New York has been good for us, but it has destroyed your father. I am so proud of you for getting good grades, and being a good young man. Your abuela would be proud too." I smile at her. My abuela, which means grandmother, passed way four months ago; she worked all her life until she came to New York.

My dad goes out a lot. So, I woke up with my dad gone. He probably went out to go get wasted at some bar in New York. My mother was in the bathroom doing her hair. Her hair was brown with long curls that flowed nicely with a fresh-cut bang in the front. They glistened against her beautiful Puerto Rican skin. "I love you, good morning," she said.

CHAPTER 3

Night Life

My ice cream in the blue bowel looks like large mountains of white clouds, melting as I eat them. My mother hears a hard knock on the door. "Let me in, come on...open the door," said my father. I recognize his voice. "Hurry, get in your room, go watch TV. Go!" said my mother firmly. My mother's voice goes from soft to hard, and then strict. Therefore, I followed her orders. "Go away Alex," she says. "Huh," he huffs and then yells, "come on!" Therefore, my mother opens the door. I could hear the door opening from my room even though the basketball game was loud. "What do you want?" she asked. "I want to be here," he said. "No you can't! I won't allow it," she said. "Come on man," he said annoyed. "No Alex good night," she said. "Huh," he huffs again. "Go sober up, then you can come in," she said. Then he walks away.

By the time they stop talking, I am in bed catching the third half of the game. After putting on my pajamas, I feel like my mother treats me as if I am little again. But in these instances, I know she was being protective of me because of what was going on so I can't be mad about that.

CHAPTER 4

A Little Love

A little love is what I needed, and I got it from Talia. She lives up the block from me; she is Columbian, and she's very pretty. She and I began talking, and then we got dared to take the big step by Chico Kayos. He dared us and questioned me, "You gonna do it man...huh?" I could hear his slick cool voice over throw my thoughts. I have to ask her," I said. He quickly replied, "Aw man...really?" He said annoyed with me and a little pissed off. "Yes, it's called respect, ask a woman before doing something," I said. It was obvious Chico was lacking that. "Okay, do what you got to do man," he said huffing.

On Tuesday, I asked her, and she said yes. By Thursday, it was the day that my hands were shaking and were sweaty. Chico was outside on the stoop smoking, and I asked him for one to calm me down. I felt mellow after, but I was still scared.

We went in her house to the bathroom and started kissing. Then I pulled out my private part and in an hour later, it was over. We did it; I was scared to ask her how she felt. I wanted to pretend I never did it, even though that was not true anymore. We did what Chico wanted, and I never felt so stupid in my life. However, we had to because it was a dare, and that's what comes with it.

CHAPTER 5

Consequences

I walked back home feeling dirty, and a shamed even though it was good, and I liked it. The whole thing still seemed dirty. So I jumped into the shower washing it all off, I thought inside my head. I just washed not even looking at my body, and trying not to look at the area past my belly...that sinful area. I got out wrapped myself in a towel, later watched TV, and ate left over's until my mother came in. She was on a late-night task.

A few days ago, three guys had got shot. Therefore, my mother had to write a front-page article on it. I wondered if she would shoot me mentally when she finds out that I had sex for the first time, and that I was dreading it too. Also, would she have me apologize to Talia for treating her like property; a sexual prop and not a young woman? Would she call me a sick bastard over this? Saying to me, "You bastard, you know better." In addition, cussing at me in Spanish telling me to shut up and not speak. What would she do...I thought?

CHAPTER 6

Calm My Mind

I waited for her to come from her job. I hear the door hiss open. She says hello to me, and I say hi back with my voice quivering.

Before I went home, I decided to take another risk on the way. Trying to block out my feelings, I had already smoked a cigarette before having intimacy with Talia. I asked Chico for some weed. I am the type of person who has to block stuff out other ways to keep me calm, which is not the best thing to do.

I am high as hell walking back, and I am amazed that I did not get hit by something. I do not smell like marijuana anymore because I took a shower. But, I accidentally left my dirty weed smelling clothes in there. My mother is headed towards the bathroom. Therefore, I try to run behind her, but I fell on the floor. I can't get up because it was a hard fall. I am paralyzed on the ground by the fall. She picks up my clothes and smells them for dirt; it is what she always does but this time I am scared. She calls me by my nickname and asked, "Javh, why do these smell like cannabis?" I pause trying to lie saying I walked pass someone who was smoking it out in the open. But I can tell she knows that I am lying. "Weed is not like cigarettes, bad excuse," she says, "you have a serious problem, how many times have you done this?" I can't answer her. "Well?" she said. She is waiting for my response. "I feel sorry for you; we make sure you are good, and all you want to do is this?" she said, "I don't know what you and I will do about this? Go to your room and think about how not to come home high as hell."

CHAPTER 7

Rehab

She whispers to me and wakes me up early, "Javh get up." I follow her into the kitchen, and I sit down. It is 6 AM, what the heck could she want to tell me unless someone has died? "I have decided you will go to Kalzon Center; it's a little ways from here; it's in Manhattan. It's a decent and nice place," she said. I roll my eyes as she talks. But she is so busy blabbing that she doesn't see me do it. She continues, "You will be there for three weeks. I have already packed your stuff, and they have activities that will keep you preoccupied like table tennis, basketball, a TV area, art gallery, art class and much more." I huff at her. "Hey you got yourself here, don't be mad at me...you caused this, not me," she says, "get up and take a bath, and then we leave."

She drags my heavy suitcase to the car, our black van. So, I do what I am told. I get into the car, and on the way there, I have Jimi Hendrix's playing on my headphones. You know the big large recording studio type ones; yeah, I have them. Purple Haze is blasting in them, and I feel sick. I heard withdrawal make you think you will die, or like you're mentally ill, even though you're not.

We walk in, and I am met at the door; they are silver colored, and you have to open them from a long metal handle that wraps around the door. In addition, on the sides, there are small luscious clean looking flowers, and small sections of grass. I guess to make it lively and pretty...I think? The director gives me a tour; it's nice. The rooms are alone like a hotel; I like that. One thing is for sure, no one is getting in this shit unless they're security, or they have control people that come in and check on you. I can actually say I like it here.

Just hours after my mother had dropped me off, we ate dinner. They brought out French fries and burgers. I can eat anywhere that I want, so I choose to eat in the area with the artwork on the wall. I like the art in the Gallery Room it is colorful; I am looking at a piece of art done by Jean-Michel Basquiat. Apparently, this place has so much freaken' money, because they got an art piece before it even came out to the public, and other 1985 art too. However, I am really into his. I wish I could do that.

I go to bed at eight, and I don't complain. I haven't made any friends yet, and wondering whether anyone will visit. But I like it, and the beds are comfortable too.

CHAPTER 8

The Pits

I woke up tossing to each side, and then I finally got up, and I sat up straight in bed. I was breathing heavy as if I had a nightmare, even though I didn't. I put on my light-gray slippers with the fluffy dark gray on the outsides and insides to keep my feet warm.

It's 8:30 AM, I shuffled to the kitchen to go get a white plastic bowl and spoon for myself. Kids are in line and at tables, they are pretty much everywhere, and adults are around them. You could easily tell the adult staff from the kids because they had on colored shirts; the men were wearing blue-green, and the females were wearing hot pink mixed with red. All I had on was my white shirt, with my dark-blue sweat pants, and my slippers to tell me apart from the millions of people here. Therefore, I locked my door before going to breakfast...smart move of mine.

I grabbed a chair; I am sitting at the head of the table with one of the male staff, and I feel so important. In China, if you sit at the head of the table, you are considered great and special. Too bad this is not China.

I continued eating my breakfast, which was Frosted Flakes, bacon, and orange juice. After that, I went to use the bog also known as the toilet to wash my hands, and then I came back out to the dining room and waited until it was time to go. Then I heard a male's voice over a microphone announcing saying, "OKAY YOU

WILL LEAVE BY GROUPS, TWO KIDS WITH A STAFFER!!!" I think whoever he is; he's using a mega phone to amplify himself because he was loud.

I get dressed; I have a green shirt with a black cartoon sports car on it, jeans, and black sneakers. I decided that I wanted to go into the TV area because there are three TVs, and I can choose one.

I am beating one of the male staff members named Bob at video games. We do that all afternoon, playing rematches. He is fun, and I like him. I also feel comfortable around him. Bob told me that the next day he wanted to play me in table tennis, which was Tuesday, but I was too sick to do anything. Therefore, he came to my room to check on me. I could tell he was worried.

What happened was that they detoxed me too fast, which made me sick. Phew, it was horrible...the pits! If anything else, it's retching getting sick with cold sweats.

By Thursday, I felt like myself, and we were ready to play table tennis.

Chapter 9

I Don't Care

I get up the next day, and I don't feel like getting dressed. Therefore, I walked around with gray sweat pants, and a dark-blue long-sleeve shirt. Now, I really felt like a bum...a drug addict. The detoxing was so bad, and it felt as if I was on heroin, even though I wasn't. I shifted my body, walking slowly, like the living dead. My body feels bad, but my mind is good. "Hey it's Bob," someone yells, and I get happy. "Hey, how you doing?" he asks. I like how he is so attentive to my needs.

Then Bob and I went to play table tennis; I passed him the small ball, and we were having fun. But about after an hour, we stopped and walked outside to sit and talk. "So, I heard you had a rough time," he said. "Yes, I did; I had no clue it was so awful. I really miss my block. I made a vow to myself not to be around Chico again. He is the reason I am here now," I replied to the counselor. I was reflecting on all my anger towards Chico; when I actually threw a drug induced temper tantrum in his office. I threw his papers on the ground, kicked over a stool, and slammed the door. He banned me from the office. But, that wasn't me, I was high...I repeat over again that was not me.

Now, every time the guard sees me at the door, he follows me back outside. It's like I am being watched all over. As far as I am concerned, that guard can suck it. I don't care, like I said it wasn't me.

I secretly relapsed that day; I was so up there I couldn't remember. When I asked why? They told me what I did, and since then I am sticking to my story. It was not me!

Chapter 10

That's All

I relapsed last Friday because I was stressed. I missed Talia and my mother, and didn't know what to do that day. I was bored, so I went outside in a hidden bush and smoked it up. Then I waltzed back inside swaying my arms like I was the man. They said I sat down on the wooden floor and wouldn't get up. They asked me to get up, but I said nothing. This one kid even kicked me...still nothing. When they pulled me up, I kicked them in the ankle and started running. They had three guards follow me down the halls. After that, I got detained and sent to my room; and that's was all. That's it? I thought. I got in trouble for that? I should have got it for my fit in that office; not this. I kicked some guard, and ran around like a five-year-old. That's all. And I get detained like I messed up this whole facility. Crazy? I am behaved now.

CHAPTER 11

Laced Libras

I am much cooler now; I am well mannered according to Mrs. Berry, the staff advisor. She made me two boxes of cupcakes for being well behaved. I shared them with Bob, and a few other kids whom I liked. We ate them in a secret area; and I have been good ever since.

I had to draw yesterday outside on a big canvas. I made an abstract piece; just Mrs. Ramona (the art teacher) and I. Mrs. Ramona is really good at art.

Now today, right this second, I am eating chips and two hot dogs, while figuring out what I want to do after lunch is done. My art piece is finished, and I took a photo of it. Then I went out and played basketball with three other guys whom I saw walking outside.

We started the game; I bounced the ball trying to do a cross over to my teammate. I dribbled the ball, and did a hook shot to the rim of the net, and it goes in. It was the third round of three games, with the Hot Suns and us. We were called the Laced Libras, which included me. We won against the Hot Suns. Laced Libras Go! We were on point that day.

CHAPTER 12

Three Weeks Already?

It has been three weeks already. Wow, that was fast. I think I am oddly enough, rather attached to this place; no matter how weird and crazy that may sound. It turns out Bob lives forty-five minutes away from me in Fort Green. He said now that Kalzon was over for me, he would be my sobriety counselor. I accepted his offer; after all, I do need it.

I spent the last week taking it all in, and building a long documented film of this place in my mind. I made friends with the kids whom I played ball with too. They don't live that far either; they live by the park I go to, which is three blocks down. It's like God is making it so that we are convenient to each other.

CHAPTER 13

Back Home Magic

I am back home; my mother got me from the center. A week later, I had a meeting with Bob for the first time. It was good; I am staying on track. I am proud of myself, and my mother is too. She's glad her Hijo is good and sober, and is taking it seriously grabbing life by the horns.

I met Talia today, she wanted to talk to me outside of the building one week after I am home. I waited around on the green bench in front of the buildings in the park. A few minutes' later, I looked up, and there she was. She was standing there with her tall body with long jet-black hair down her back, her light beautiful Columbian skin, and her pretty hot pink nails. Her polished hands touch my hand, and then she opened her mouth to speak and said, "Hi." I paused, and then said Hi back as my voice was quivering. "Look," I said. Then she interrupts me and said, "I know you went on a trip, and I know what we did. But while you were on your trip, I thought about everything, and I like you." She pauses waiting for my response. "But my issues, it will mess stuff up," I said as I stumbled over my words. "No it won't," she said. I fired back, "Yes it will!" She is a bit startled, but then she simmers back down. "Because," she said to me sweet and calmly unlike I was able to do, "because I love you regardless." I huffed in annoyances. She continues and said, "Because I like who you are. I love you for you. I love and like you, whether you're in your issues or not. I like you period beyond all that, and I am with you regardless." After her long drawn-out speech, I said slowly and basic, "Okay." Then she turns my face towards her, and we kissed. I am beginning to really like her, and she's a good kisser. Her kisses were like fireworks, and I am glad she has my back. That makes guys really feel girls when they have your back.

CHAPTER 14

Artwork of the Heart

I called Talia on the house phone. My mother is in the bathroom curling her hair with the big rollers. You know the ones that look similar to toilet paper rolls. Talia agrees to meet my mother and I at the art museum. I will be excited to see the art, but I hope they have the artist there. I like the artist whose artwork is displayed at the Kalzon Center. I am now a huge fan of Jean-Michel Basquiat, and I can't wait to get to the art museum to see Talia.

The cab comes towards us, and we took it to the museum. Talia and I are laughing while looking at things out the window from the back of the cab. My mother says that she has something to tell me, a surprise.

When we got to the museum, and we looked at all the art. I got excited when I saw Jean's art. I looked at it intently, and immerse myself in it. I can tell my mother is happy to see me having excitement all over on my face.

Afterwards, we went to lunch; I ate a sandwich and drank a cola. Talia orders a tuna melt and juice. My mother orders soup and chips. My mother gets up from the table, pulls me to the side and says, "Hijo, your father and I are getting back together." I look confused. "I don't think that's a good Idea," I tell my mother boldly. She looks down being unsure. "He went to counseling, and had rehab the same time as you. He has changed," she said. I ignore her as she talks, still not convinced.

We are now walking back to the apartment. Talia and I are talking in the back of my mother as she walks ahead of us. As we lag behind, I see my dad on the side of my mother walking, and I pause. He hugs my mother, and then she shifts the focus to him saying hello to Talia, who is my girlfriend. She nicely greets him and then I looked at him. And I saw what my mother was saying was true. Therefore, I hugged my dad so tight. Then we did a group hug all together.

CHAPTER 15

Unlike Me

I ate my eggs and bacon as I looked at it on the plate. My father has Louis Armstrong on. I looked at him like, since when did he like jazz or that type of music? I hear it in the background of this part of my life right now. I heard he also smoked quite a bit of marijuana. Unlike me, he just let it ride in his life; and I am not doing it anymore. I told myself that it was good when I lit it up and got a hyper rush from it. I got a coolness, a mellow vibe from the middle part. Then by the end, it's dead. It has died, and I am back. Back to me or whatever that was. But him, he just did his thing. He didn't get busted out there like Billie Holiday, or any other famous drug users at that time. But like I said that's it's not for me. I'm not saying I could never relapse, but honestly before that day ever happens, I am going to try so hard until my hands scar.

There is something with my father. I called him my father, but before that, he was just dad, boring and a moldy long. But now, I call him and can call him father. He told me about sobriety, and I am sticking to it. I'm proud of him now.

CHAPTER 16

Poor Chico

I am outside getting a cool breeze. I am by myself; Talia is out with her mother Mrs. Lula Diaz, who is very friendly. I am completely into myself in this moment. Then I looked to my side, and there was Chico Kayos. I am trying not to look him in the eye as he comes towards me. I am panicking all around me. It's like the drug addicts with no money to pay. He sees me, and I play it cool. "Hey," he said. I try not to look up, but his slick voice over shadows me again. "Hi," I replied. "You want to smoke it?" Chico asked. "Naw man," I said. He looks like he's going to beat the shit out of me, the same way like a normal drug deal does. But he doesn't, instead he takes a deep cool breath. Then he said something shocking, "I'm proud of you man. You got guts; I don't have any. See you around, you're one of my true friend's man." Chico waves his hand up to me, and I waved back to him. I then thought to myself, "I guess I can be his friend." I saw that he was feeling good. However, that was the last time I saw him.

Two weeks later, he was dead. Chico was shot in a drug scuffle; he was only nineteen. I was shocked at how heartbroken I was about it.

Talia and I went to his funeral; he had a big family. His mother and father cry all the time, and I feel so bad for them. He is in my mind all the time; his voice is prevalent in my thoughts. He was good beyond what my mother calls forced. Forced is something that is not the true you, but is a creation of something else. That was Chico, he was forced.

CHAPTER 17

Cool Pool

It's hot this day; it's the annoying humid sticky stick to your skin hot. I hate that kind of heat, and you sweat more with that.

Talia and I decided to take a cab; she had her bathing suit, and I had my swimming trunks. We got inside the cab, and we drove to an indoor swimming place. We had both a swimsuit and swim shoes.

Talia first jumped in splashing and everything, and then I did. I then started laughing in the water. Then we started dunking each other in the water until both of us were under water holding our breaths. Our hairs were waving like mermaids, and waving at each other. It was holding hands towards each other under water, and then we splashed each other. Talia was laughing the entire time; her laugh is beautiful.

We dried off and changed our clothes. Then we put the wet bathing suits in large white towels, and went back home to watch TV in the living room. The basketball game is on, so we both yelled at the TV while cozying up with each other. I want to go swimming with her again; it was really fun for me.

CHAPTER 18

Funny Nights

I saw Talia from the window, and I waved at her. She also sees me, and waves back. Therefore, I motioned for her to come up to the building, and she does. Then I hear the elevator door beep, and I see her on the side of me as I look out the large window in the hall with the elevator. You can see everyone from the ground in the windows view.

I invite Talia inside. I go get my light fleece jacket; that's dark blue with light blue buttons. Talia has one too; it's black with a fake light fur collar.

We walk up the stairs to the building's roof, and then we sit down and talk. "What was Kalzon like?" she asked. "It was hard at first, the schedule I had to get use to it. And when I got sick from cleaning up. Phew, you have no idea it was awful," I said. "Wow," she said and then she paused scratching her long hair. "Hey I am having a family dinner tonight want to come?" I asked. "Yes, if it's alright with your mother," she said. "Yes, it is. I asked her already when you were sitting on the couch," I responded.

By eight thirty, Talia was at my door, and I welcomed her in like a gentleman. "Hello my lady," I said all proper, and she giggled. "your throne awaits," I continued, and she giggled again as she found her seat at the table.

When we were seated, we ate rice, chicken, mixed vegetables, and for desert chocolate Boston Cream Pie. After we ate, we watched basketball. Talia sat with me on one seat together; we were squashed together, but comfortable.

We were watching the game, and I fell down laughing. Talia is nervous because I am screaming and laughing on the floor. But then, she realizes why my father's face of sports disappointment is too funny. His face is like how could you be so stupid, and he is snarling like a little dog, which makes it funny because it's all loud, and it's a supper funny sound. We both end up laughing so hard on the floor. It was a great night, and too funny.

CHAPTER 19

School Time

It's school time again for me, I got reintegrated into school after being at Kalzon for a long time. I feel reintegrated means to show up again.

I met Talia downstairs to walk her to school. She and I go to the same school; she just got in. It's her second day there. For me, it's my first time back in a long time.

We walked three long blocks *(we are walking with hot cream cheese bagels)* and on the way, I am telling Talia that I am going to hide myself. She looks at me strange and says, "That's dumb? Why don't you just show yourself?" I thought about what she just said, and she's right; it is dumb. I am not a criminal, so why not show myself. I feel weird now. "That was dumb," I replied. "Yeah it was," she says.

I held and clutched her hand tighter as we were passing a few cars on the street. We ended up at the school. It is this square tall building that is a chocolate brown, and has blue doors and blue window frames. We walked in and went to our classes, and then we saw each other again at lunch. I ate with her, and I asked her how she likes it so far. She goes on and on about the classes, and some of the wild crazy but funny bad behaving kids in her English class. We both ate turkey and cheese sandwiches, and drank water to keep us up. I will see her again at the last class of the day, which is Art.

There is a lady there, but I can't recognize her. I think I know her, but can't seem to put a name to her face. As she turns around, she shouts my name in excitement, "Javio!" I smile because now I know who she is; it's Mrs. Ramona from Kalzon. *She must work here;* I thought in my mind.

She motions me over to hug her. She gives me this large sweet bear hug. I listen as she teaches she says, "Next week we will work." Talia and I leave school and walk home while the other kids wait for busses or their mothers, like I use to do.

When we got back to the apartment, we did some math. But while there, we decided to go get food because it's a little late, and we're hungry. Her mother gave her twenty dollars, so we ordered fries, burgers, and two milkshakes. We ate until we were content, and then sat in a park nearby. There are lots of little kids running around with their parents, we found a spot on one bench and watched them play, and also watched the New York Sky Line. We left early to get home.

CHAPTER 20

Great Read

I awaken to see books on my nightstand. It's Saturday, yesterday was Friday; and I see books. I picked up two books in my hands, there is one about people, or should I say writers in Latina literature, and another about Malcolm X. I find both covers interesting. However, I decided to leave them where they were, puzzled and worried that I could get someone upset by moving them.

I walked around the apartment in early morning, and I see my mother. She is getting dressed to go out to do a little trip to the store, she also says she is making pancakes. Therefore, I ask her as she grabs her jacket to go to the store down the street, "Who bought me these books?" "Your father, he thought you might like them," she answered. I walk in their bedroom; my father is in a deep sleep in the bed. My mother side is unmade, because she just got up. His mouth is closed; his right hand is over his head, and his long hair is neatly trimmed down. When I saw him, he woke up. He is groggy, making noises, and turning his back to me. I am sitting on a small couch across the room. It's one of those old 1970s type of couches with a tan wood outside base where you put a type of mattress in it, and have it upright looking like a couch. Yeah, they have that one.

He wakes up, by this time I am on the couch in the spacious living room watching TV. I say, thank you to him, and he says you're welcome, and that both books are a great read.

CHAPTER 21

My Grandfather

Today is the day my grandfather does his annual check in. He's socially, active in our family; and he's aware of everything. However, he's also the type of man who is engaged in family life heavily, and then goes off for a while to focus on himself. That's the type of man Ramon Gualdez is. That's my grandfather, he is tough, but sweet, a Columbian man who grew up a hard worker. By the age of ten, he was rescued in the 1940s from forced child work labor. His parents went with him to the United States, and that's where they have been since then. His parents died a few years back.

I heard the doorbell ring; my mother answers the door. "Abuelo," she says as she hugs him, "come...come in. Want something to drink?" "Yes," he said. As he waited, I said, "Hello Abuelo." I shook his hand firmly. "Oh, you thought that Hijo Espanola," he said in his thick but easy to understand Columbian accent. My mother laughed and said, "Sí my grandfather asked me, have you been staying sober? "Yes, I have," I said. "What about you, Alex?" he asked. My father said, "Yes." My grandfather paused then said, "Well good." After that, they had water, and some light food like burritos, and light fluffy eggs with turkey. It was morning, I forgot to say that. But it was a good visit from my Abuelo. He has wisdom from learning things.

CHAPTER 22

Brazil Planes

It's hot outside, and the air is warm. It reminds me of Brazil in the spring, and the area I know of that has planes flying over it constantly. They're so loud you can't talk until it goes away. But this is not my home country; this is New York City; a plane only goes by once in a blue moon. Not constantly, unless you live next to JFK airport, which I don't. It would be too loud anyway. I can already think about how bad that would be if my mother had to yell over the large planes. In addition, use a type of physical language to let me know what she said. It would be similar to sign language, and Talia would have to pull my arm along with her where we have to go, because I cannot hear her. This would hurt me because she would pull it like pulling a long heavy rope. Nevertheless, that rope would be my arm, half-broken and overly sore. I would lose my mind if I lived close to that. No offences to people who do. But not me...no way! Therefore, I am glad I live where I do. Even though the planes come once in a blue moon. But I do miss the sky-high planes of Brazil.

CHAPTER 23

Accents

I am sleeping it's the early morning; my feet are dangling off the bed, and the fan is going in my room as I lay on the light-blue blanket with the sown ends dangling down. My face is planted on the side of this blanket. I hear a knock; it's my mother she's calling me in her usual tone I think in a Spanish accent, "Hijo get up." Her accent is ringing in my ear. I am wondering what she wants me to do today. Her voice sounds muffled through the door. Now she is cussing in Espanola at me. Her accent rolling off her tongue, it's like a dog licking itself constantly. I follow her orders, and do whatever she wants.

CHAPTER 24

Blue House

I remember the Blue House in my dreams, especially how it looks and smells. It smells like hot dust, a cool rainfall, and sometimes flowers. However, that was rare. In many ways, the house is like me. It has different moods and behaviors. The house is me, and I am the house. And as crazy as that may sound, I don't miss the house. However, sometimes I do when I reminisce about the Orange Farm with the sweet oranges, and the dust caked in the ground by cars passing the main lonely road of Coinchia.

Coinchia is the town where we lived; Coinchia was beautiful, but I could only enjoy some things about it. It was like enjoying the sun for two minutes, and then being forced to leave. That was Coinchia for me. It was a place that I rarely got to enjoy; the full life of it, and its glory (full town of beauty).

CHAPTER 25

Everything's Good

It is Saturday night, and the New York streets have a hint of glowing light in the dismal rainy air due to the rain. Talia and I decided to see a movie. My mother is with us; she promised me that she will sit in the back; but not too far so, she can still keep a close eye on us. We find our seats passing people in rows, and Talia is right behind me trying to keep up as if her life depended on us sticking close. Like those movies where you stay with each other or one will die, like a horror film. That's Talia's domineer at the seat moving. We finally get comfortable sitting in our seats. I have the big bucket of popcorn. My mother got two; one for us, and one for herself. So I am here with this bucket of popcorn on my lap, and Talia is next to me. We get bored by the infomercials with the stupid songs and ads about this and that. There are no movie ads playing yet, so due to boredom we decided to make some noise. We started having a popcorn fight, and laughing. It's getting on people nerves; therefore, we stopped after an annoyed older man in his forty's tells us to shut up, whispering it to himself. Then the movie starts. Right at this moment, I am thinking about everything I have been through, like a rewound tape in my mind. And I came to the conclusion that I will put my thoughts on hold, because I am about to watch this movie that I wanted to see for weeks. Furthermore, I am sober now; I have my girlfriend, and this popcorn. So I think everything's good.

ABOUT THE AUTHOR

Zaire Hodges is writer and a published author. Her debut novel titled The Rhythm of Poetry was published on September 13, 2012.

The Blue House on the Left – A Novel is her recent work. This is the author's first raw, and no holds bar piece of literature that she has done. You can find her books on most online bookstores, including Amazon, and Barnes and Noble.

Thank you in advance for your support and enjoy!
Zaire

www.ingramcontent.com/pod-product-compliance
Lightning Source LLC
Chambersburg PA
CBHW070420120726
47909CB00005B/1724